I dedicate this book to my lovely husband John.
Also, my children Rachelle, James and Samantha, and
grandchildren, Isabel, Katy, Jessica, Charles and
Maximus, who have all played on Little Rusty Tractor.

Acknowledgements

I would like to say thank you to Mick and Jim Dutton for the wonderful restoration they did on our precious little Massey Ferguson 35X Tractor.

A big thank you to my son-in-law Simon Gray for his encouragement, help and guidance.

A special thank you to everyone who has worked on the book, Kate Smith and her team, Helen Graper, Marketa Rams, Juliana Bentley and Sophie Cartmell for the amazing illustrations that have brought my story to life.

Published by New Generation Publishing in 2016

Text Copyright © Jacky Cripwell 2016

Illustrations Copyright © Kate Smith 2016

Photography Copyright © Sammy Smiles Photograpy 2016

First Edition

ISBN 978-1-78507-842-2

www.newgeneration-publishing.com

Little Rusty Tractor's Big Day!

by Jacky Cripwell

Based on a true story...

Illustrated by Kate Smith

Once upon a time, in a country village called Bunny, past the church and down the lane there was a small farm. The farm belonged to a farmer whose grandchildren called him 'Grumpy'.

Grumpy loved his farm and all the animals.
He had three pet sheep called Lottie, Aggie and Cherry.
There was also a paddock with a pond where
geese and chickens lived.

Grumpy had a large shed where he kept all of his farm machinery. Inside, was Big Green Tractor and very, very old Little Rusty Tractor.

Big Green Tractor was always busy out in the field.
In spring, Grumpy used him to plant seeds,
and at the end of the day he was put back in the shed where he
would tell Little Rusty Tractor all about his many adventures.

In early summer, Big Green Tractor was used for hay making.
After a hard day at work, Big Green Tractor would tell
Little Rusty Tractor about all of the exciting
things he'd been up to.

Little Rusty Tractor spent her days gazing out of the shed.
In summer, she could see bees buzzing and butterflies fluttering.
She wished she could be out doing something useful like
her friend Big Green Tractor. Little Rusty Tractor
began to feel lonely and sad.

It was harvest time and Big Green Tractor had his busiest time ever. He had to cart the corn from the combine harvester to the corn merchants, he worked all day and sometimes all night.

When Big Green Tractor returned home to the shed,
he couldn't wait to tell his friend about the
wonderful time he'd had and all the
wildlife he had seen.

Little Rusty Tractor was pleased to see her friend,
but she still felt very sad as she wished she could
go out and do some work, too.

Autumn came and all the leaves were turning a lovely shade of golden brown. Big Green Tractor was out getting the soil ready for winter crops, but when he returned home, much to his dismay Little Rusty Tractor was gone!

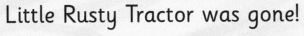

Big Green Tractor missed his friend – he had no
one to share his stories with anymore.
He now felt sad and lonely, just as
Little Rusty Tractor had done so often.

Every day Big Green Tractor returned from
work hoping to see his friend,
but Little Rusty Tractor was nowhere to be seen.

It was now winter; snow had started to fall, and it had become extremely cold. While Grumpy's grandchildren Isabel, Katy and Jessica played in the snow and built a snowman, Grumpy spent the day chopping logs, ready to take into the house to make a nice warm fire.

Big Green Tractor stayed in the shed,
as there wasn't a lot of work for him to do in winter.
He was so lonely and missed his friend
Little Rusty Tractor more than ever.

Eventually, the snow melted and spring returned.
Winter was finally over. Suddenly Big Green Tractor
could hear a familiar noise coming through the yard,
it was his old friend Little Rusty Tractor.

But wait! She was not old Little Rusty Tractor anymore, she looked as good as new! Her bright red paint gleamed and her headlights sparkled in the sunshine. Big Green Tractor was so happy to see his friend home .

WOW! Hello!

Early next morning, Grumpy walked over to the shed at the start of a very special day. He sat on Little Rusty Tractor's new seat and started the engine — it hummed perfectly.

Outside the shed was a trailer decorated with beautiful flowers. Grumpy hitched the trailer to the back of Little Rusty Tractor and tied some white ribbon to her bonnet. She looked magnificent!

This was a very special day for Grumpy – his daughter Samantha was getting married. It meant the world to Samantha to have the tractor she loved so much as a little girl, take her to the church.

Little Rusty Tractor was driven through the village and everybody looked and cheered. Little Rusty Tractor was so proud – what a wonderful day!

That night, Grumpy parked Little Rusty Tractor next
to her friend Big Green Tractor.
Now it was Little Rusty Tractor's turn to tell
the story of her exciting day, and
Big Green Tractor was all ears!

Editor's Blurb

In the country village of Bunny, there was a small farm that belonged to a farmer whose Grandchildren call him Grumpy. On his farm, he had a large shed, and inside were two tractors: Big Green Tractor and Little Rusty Tractor. Poor old Little Rusty Tractor had been left in the shed for years, while Big Green Tractor spent most of his days on the farm with Grumpy.

One day, Big Green Tractor came back to the shed after a day's work, and was ready to tell Little Rusty Tractor all about his adventures, but she was nowhere to be seen. Where had she gone?

All Little Rusty Tractor wished for was to be useful again just like her friend Big Green Tractor. Then one special day, her dreams came true.

About the Author

Jacky is originally from Cheshire. She met and married John, a farmer in Bunny and has lived there for over 30 years, their three children grew up on the farm and have shared many happy times.

The motivation for her to write this story came from her young grandson Charlie. As a toddler he spent a lot of time with her and liked to help clean the goose hut out and collect the eggs, but most of all he loved to sit on Little Rusty Tractor. The other grandchildren enjoyed listening to all the stories that happened on the farm. Jacky always wanted to share the true tales of the wonderful time on the farm so they will never be forgotten.

To see some of the real-life characters on Grumpy's Farm please visit facebook.com/grumpysfarmbooks

Charlie driving Little Rusty Tractor

Big Green Tractor and Little Rusty Tractor with John and Jacky Cripwell